BREAKING THE SILENCE

A Teen's Journey Through Bullying, Love,
and Overcoming the Trials of Life

James Vision Jacobs

Archway Publishing books may be ordered through booksellers or by contacting:

Archway Publishing
1663 Liberty Drive
Bloomington, IN 47403
www.archwaypublishing.com
844-669-3957

Interior Image Credit: James Vision Jacobs

ISBN: 978-1-6657-4006-7 (sc)
ISBN: 978-1-6657-4007-4 (e)

Library of Congress Control Number: 2023904074

Print information available on the last page.

Archway Publishing rev. date: 01/15/2025

I want to express my gratitude to God first for allowing me to align with his vision and allowing me to share my passions with the world!

My heartfelt appreciation goes out to my beautiful daughters, Noelle, Jasmine, and Jordan, who have grown into remarkable young women. Your unwavering support and unwavering belief in me have given me the strength to persevere and overcome every obstacle. I am grateful for your presence in my life, and I am immensely proud of you and I will love you forever.

A huge Thank you to my brothers, Joe, Kevin, Lamar, Jermaine, and Kenny, for their unwavering support and love. Your constant encouragement and loyalty have been the cornerstone of my success, and I cherish each one of you. You all hold a special place in my heart, and I will love you till the end of time.

I dedicate this book to my father, Joe Green, who was my first inspiration in the world of art. Your strength and skills, which God chose to pass on to me, have been the foundation of my artistic journey. Though you are no longer with us, I know that you are still guiding us and helping us achieve our dreams. I promise to use the gifts you have given me to impact the world positively. I will always be indebted to you for your wisdom and insight.

Finally, I want to express my deepest appreciation to my mother, Wendy Green Jacobs, whose unwavering love and dedication have been the driving force behind my success. Your selflessness and kindness inspire me to be a better person every day. You are the epitome of grace and resilience, and I am blessed to have you as my mother. Thank you for being the greatest woman I have ever known.

"The Toilet Bowl Tomb"

John stood at the sink, staring at his reflection in the mirror as the sounds of Odell's taunts and the toilet bowl swirling filled his ears. He closed his eyes and wished for it all to be over, for the toilet bowl to truly become his tomb. It was a weekly ritual, one that he had endured since middle school, and one that he hoped would end soon. The toilet bowl had become his mental jail cell which he allowed Odell to put him in it and keep the key. Every day John asked himself when would it end.

Even as he stood there, feeling the water on his face and the teasing words in his ears, he couldn't help but think back to how he had gotten to this point.

Growing up, John's life had not been easy. His family was poor and his father was struggling with addiction, rarely present in his life. John's mother worked hard to provide for him and the household, and their relationship was close despite the challenges they faced.

But at school, John faced a different set of challenges. He was teased for his clothes, his hair, and the fact that he received free lunch in school instead of buying it like the other students. He had the same backpack he had started elementary school with, and it often led to mocking and ridicule.

Visions Of Faith are what he needed to confront the challenges at a young age. The worst injustice John faced was at the hands of Odell, the school bully. Odell made it his daily mission to torment and humiliate him in new and creative ways. The toilet bowl swirlies were a classic, one that John dreaded every week.

As John stood in the bathroom with water dripping from his face, he made a silent vow to himself, recalling his mother's words about being transformed by "The Renewing of our Minds." He realized that every thought could be held captive when it didn't align with the word of God. He wouldn't let Odell or anyone else break him. He wouldn't let the toilet bowl be his tomb. Instead, he would rise above it all and succeed. Despite everything, John held onto hope. He knew that one day, he would escape the confines of poverty and the cruelties of school life. He would make something of himself, rise above it all, and prove everyone wrong who had ever doubted or mistreated him.

"The Bully and the Betrayed"

Odell was a bully, there was no denying that. He was held back a couple grades, so it was easy for him to bully other kids. He took pleasure in tormenting and belittling others, and John was one of his primary targets. But what few people knew was that Odell was also being tormented.

At home, Odell faced physical abuse from his mother's new boyfriend Kevin and was subjected to the horrors of violence and alcohol-induced torture. It was possible that Odell's own experiences with abuse and oppression had led him to bully others, like John.

Meanwhile, John struggled with his own set of issues. His relationship with his father was strained due to his addiction and absence from John's life. John often felt angry and betrayed by his father and struggled with whether or not he wanted him to be a part of his life. He had enough to deal with at school, without also having to worry about his father's problems.

But as the two boys faced their own demons, they were also connected by their shared experiences of pain and hardship. While they may have been on opposite ends of the bullying dynamic, they both knew what it was like to feel powerless and alone.

A popular song by Michael Jackson was called "Man in the Mirror." The song encouraged anyone can change their lives. And as they navigated their difficult lives, they couldn't help but wonder what the future held for them. Would they be able to rise above their circumstances and find a way out of the cycle of abuse and oppression? Or would they be doomed to repeat the same patterns of hurt and hurt again?

"The Power of Education"

Despite the many challenges he faced at home and at school, John excelled in his studies. He knew that education was his key to breaking the cycle of poverty and social inequality that had plagued his family for generations. His mother frequently encouraged him to take his studies seriously, reminding him that a good education held the promise of a better life.

And John was determined not to let anything stand in the way of his goals. He worked hard every day, pouring over his textbooks and completing his assignments to the best of his ability. He excelled in subjects like math and science, always eager to learn more and expand his knowledge.

But it wasn't just his grades that set John apart. He was also a natural leader, always willing to stand up for what he believed in and help his classmates when they needed it. He had a strong sense of justice and fairness, and he was determined to use his education to make a difference in the world.

As John progressed through high school, he began to realize that his dreams were within reach. He applied for scholarships and worked part-time to save money for college. He knew that it wouldn't be easy, but he was determined to make a better life for himself and his family.

And as he looked towards the future and maybe one day becoming a scientist, doctor, or a lawyer, he couldn't help but feel grateful for the power of education. It had given him the tools he needed to overcome his circumstances and pursue his passions. It had given him hope, and he knew that with hard work and determination, anything was possible. So, he decided to pursue his higher studies in a prestigious university and make a career out of it.

"The Comfort of Friendship"

Despite the daily struggles he faced, John found solace in the form of a pretty girl named Hannah. She had brown, curly hair, green eyes, and a smile that made the turmoil of school bearable for John. They shared classes together, and Hannah always made an effort to throw him an encouraging smile and even gave him muffins when they were alone.

It was clear to John that Hannah was different from the other kids at school. She didn't judge him based on his poverty or the clothes he wore. She seemed to genuinely care about him and his well-being, and her kindness was a beacon of light in an otherwise dark and cruel world.

As they spent more time together, John and Hannah became close friends. They talked about everything and anything, sharing their deepest hopes and fears with each other. John confided in Hannah about his troubled relationship with his father and the bullying he faced at the hands of Odell. Hannah listened patiently, offering comfort and support whenever he needed it.

And in return, John was there for Hannah as well. He learned that she too had her own set of struggles, including a strained relationship with her parents and a lack of confidence in herself. John encouraged her to pursue her passions and to never give up on her dreams.

Together, the two friends formed a bond that was unbreakable. They leaned on each other for support and comfort, and their friendship provided a sense of stability and belonging in a world that often seemed unfair and uncaring.

As John looked back on his time with Hannah, he knew that he was grateful to have her in his life. She had been a constant source of strength and support, and he knew that he would always treasure their friendship. Despite their busy schedules, they managed to keep in touch and meet each other during holidays. They remained the best of friends throughout their lives.

"The Turning Point"

John's school days were made even more difficult by Odell. He would frequently target John, giving him wedgies and swirlies whenever he had the chance. But one day, Odell noticed Hannah talking and laughing with John at his locker. Rather than acting on his usual impulses, Odell began the day chasing John in the hallway but slowed his pace and decided to come up with a more elaborate plan to torment him.

That plan came to fruition a few days later when Odell ambushed John in the bathroom. He had brought a group of his friends with him, and they surrounded John, taunting and jeering as he tried to escape.

But just as they were closing in on him, something unexpected happened. Hannah burst into the bathroom, her eyes blazing with anger. She stood between John and the bullies, her fists clenched at her sides.

"Leave him alone!" she yelled. "Don't you have any shame?"

The bullies were taken aback by Hannah's sudden appearance and her bold words. They hesitated for a moment, unsure of what to do next. And in that moment of hesitation, John saw his chance. He broke free from the circle and made a run for it, Hannah close behind him.

As they fled the bathroom, John's heart was racing. He couldn't believe what had just happened. Hannah had stood up for him, had risked her own safety to protect him. It was a moment that would change everything.

From that day on, Odell's bullying stopped. He still tried to intimidate John and Hannah on occasions, but his attacks were no longer as frequent or as severe. John and Hannah were grateful for the respite, and they knew that they owed it all to Hannah's bravery.

But more than that, they knew that they had each other's backs. They were a team, united against the cruelty of the world. And as they faced the challenges of high school together, they knew that they could overcome anything as long as they had each other.

11

"A Glimmer of Hope"

It was the end of their junior year, and John couldn't help but think about how wonderful it would be to finish high school and start a new life once he graduated. The next school year, as the school prom approached, Hannah rode her bike and stopped John on his way home, asking if he would like to go with her. John eagerly accepted, and the two made plans to attend the prom together.

John's growing relationship with Hannah represented a glimmer of hope in an otherwise difficult and tumultuous time. He felt grateful for her presence in his life and looked forward to the possibilities that lay ahead. Despite all the challenges he had faced, John remained determined to make a better life for himself and his family through education and hard work.

With Hannah, John couldn't help but feel proud of all that he had accomplished. He had overcome so much, and he knew that he had Hannah to thank for much of it. She had stood by him through thick and thin, and he knew that he could always count on her.

John couldn't help but feel a sense of hope and optimism for the future. He knew that he still had a long way to go, but he was determined to make the most of every opportunity that came his way.

On the days they hung out, he would look into Hannah's eyes, he knew that he had found something truly special. He had found a friend, a confidante, a partner in crime. He had found someone who understood him and cared about him, and he knew that he was lucky to have her by his side.

"The Darkness Within"

As the date of the prom drew closer and closer, Hannah and John spent more and more time together. They began sitting beside each other in their science and math classes and eating lunch with Hannah's friends. It was blissful, and John hadn't even been bullied by Odell in days. He was on cloud nine.

But behind the facade of Odell's bullying lay a deeper darkness. When Odell went home after football practice, he was met with a motherless house. Cowering at the possibility of being beaten for no reason, he grabbed some things from the fridge to eat and retired to his room to avoid his mother's boyfriend.

A few minutes later, a strong whiff of alcohol penetrated his room as his mother's boyfriend swung the door open. Yelling at the top of his voice, the boyfriend began beating Odell mercilessly for no reason. The ordeal ended with Odell's head resting in a small puddle of blood, his nose aching and throbbing from the abuse. His mother's boyfriend took a swig of beer and left the room, leaving Odell alone and battered.

These attacks became more and more frequent, and Odell noticed that his mother always came home after her boyfriend had "cooled down." Where was Odell's help coming from? Where was the love?

Later on, Odell would find out that his mother had been beaten by her boyfriend too, and she was afraid to stay at home. Little did she know that her boyfriend was also beating her son. No one knew that the boyfriend also suffered from anger management issues and needed professional help, but instead, he used John and his mother as outlets to take his anger out on.

In pain and trembling fear, Odell lay, paralyzed by the weight of his suffering, too afraid to confide in his mother. For her support and the stability of their household relied on the affluent embrace of her boyfriend, a man ensnared in the treacherous web of drug trade and fortune. Odell pondered, his soul heavy with bewilderment, how his life had spiraled into this desolate abyss. Once a tormentor, a bully who inflicted wounds upon others to alleviate his own inner turmoil, now he glimpsed his own reflection in their eyes—the eyes of fellow victims. Trapped within the vicious cycle of abuse and violence, his spirit yearned for liberation, yet no pathway appeared before him, shackled by the relentless grip of despair.

And as the prom approached, Odell couldn't shake the feeling that his life was spiraling out of control. He didn't know how to escape the darkness within him, and he feared that it would consume him forever.

"The Fear of Loss"

As the day came to a close, John spotted Odell at the top of the hall walking towards him. With such a good day, he decided to try his luck with his resident bully and remain still. As Odell drew closer, John noticed more and more distinct features: a blood-red nose, stitched cheek, and black eye. Odell sauntered right by John without so much as a glance, and elation washed over John in waves.

For the first time in a long time, John finally had a period of happiness. It felt as if it would never go away, but there was a looming fear in the back of his mind that it would all disappear within an instant, being much worse than it was before.

John couldn't shake the feeling that his happiness was fragile and precarious. He had been through so much in his life, and he had learned that things could change in an instant. He was constantly on edge, always fearing that the other shoe would drop and his world would come crashing down around him.

But despite this fear, John was determined to hold on to his happiness. He knew that it was something special and rare, and he was grateful for every moment of it. He vowed to never take it for granted

"The Breaking Point One"

On the day the waitlist candidates were announced for the science paper project, John arrived at school early, his heart racing with excitement and anxiety. He paced the halls, eagerly waiting for the list to be posted. As more students arrived, Hannah came up to him and asked, "So, John, are you excited?"

"I'm freaking out, Hannah," John replied. "What if we don't get it?"

"We'll get it, don't worry," Hannah assured him.

Just then, Emily, one of Hannah's friends, approached them. "Hey, all, waiting for the results?" she asked.

"Yes," John and Hannah replied in unison.

"Me too," Emily said. "I'm so excited, but I probably didn't get it."

"I'm sure you did, just wait and see," Hannah said encouragingly.

As the principal's assistant made her way to the notice board, the students crowded around her, almost trampling her in their eagerness to see the list. Once the pushpin was placed through the A4-sized paper, the students swarmed to see if their names were on it. As the crowd cleared, one disappointed student at a time, John and Hannah scanned the list, but their names were nowhere to be found.

"I don't understand," John said. "You remembered to hand it in, right?"

"Yes, John," Hannah replied. "Emily was on her way to class, so I asked her to hand it in for me. You handed it in, right, Em?"

"Yes, Odell did," Emily said.

"What?" John exclaimed.

"Well, Odell stopped me in the hall and kind of charmed me into submitting our papers for us, so I just gave them to him. Why?" Emily explained.

John's heart stopped and he was overwhelmed by waves of depression. All he could manage to say was "No." Dejected, he went home and curled up on his bed, crying indefinitely. As he lay there, he couldn't help but think about how Odell had deliberately torn up his science project and left it in his locker, the satisfaction on his face as he walked away etched in John's mind.

This betrayal was a breaking point for John. He had always tried to see the good in people, even Odell, hoping that one day he could help him see the error of his ways. But now, he realized that he had been naive. Odell was beyond redemption, and John knew that he had to distance himself from the bully or somehow stop him if he wanted to move forward with his life.

As the tears dried on his cheeks, John made a vow to himself. He would never let anyone else have that kind of power over him again. He would be strong, he would be resilient, and he would make a better life for himself and his family. And he would do it all without the help of anyone else, especially not someone like Odell.

"The Unexpected"

John felt defeated as he trudged to school that next morning, his spirits sinking even lower when he and Hannah received the grades from their science paper. They sat together in their favorite lunch spot, Hannah apologizing profusely for trusting her friend Emily with the important assignment. But Hannah had already spoken to the science teacher, who had to give them extra time to turn in their paper, the teacher also stated "the project will be graded later and will also have points deducted.

Hannah was also surprised to hear about the other years of bullying that Odell had subjected John to and not just on a few occasions, urging him to find the courage to stand up for himself. Hannah said nothing, but she knew that if John didn't take a stand and be strong, Odell would never stop, potentially destroying not only John but possibly also their relationship. By the end of lunch, Hannah had somehow managed to lift John's spirits and make him feel like a king, like everything would be okay no matter what. John left feeling on top of the world, with a chance to redo their science paper and a beautiful girl as his date for the prom. But when he arrived at his apartment building, he was greeted by the sight of police cars and an ambulance, his optimism shattering in an instant.

"The Weight of Guilt"

Fear and panic set in as John walked up the stairs to his apartment, where he found his mother sitting at the kitchen table, hunched over a mountain of bills and crying as she tried to prioritize which ones she could afford to pay that month. But John knew that there was more to her tears than just the bills and final shut-off notices. His mother, Kelly, was struggling to hide her true feelings, and she eventually told John about his father's serious car accident and his critical condition at the hospital. She had just received updates from the doctors and police, but she knew that ensuring these bills were paid was crucial. Failing to do so would only add to their existing problems and make it challenging to cover any necessary medical expenses. John's world crashed down around him as he realized that his father's accident might be his fault. He couldn't help but remember his last interaction with his father, when he had told him that he would never forgive him for abandoning him and his mother and to just stay away. John also knew that his father was a reckless, drunk driver and had always feared that something like this might happen.

The weight of guilt weighed heavy on John's shoulders on the days he sat by his father's hospital bed, watching him hooked up to machines and barely clinging to life. He couldn't help but think about all the times he had wished his father would disappear from his life, and now he was faced with the possibility of that wish becoming a reality. He felt responsible for his father's condition, and he couldn't shake the feeling that he could have done something to prevent it.

As he sat there, John made a promise to himself that he would never give up on his father, no matter how hard things got. He would be there for him, through thick and thin, and he would do whatever it took to help him recover as well as forgive him. And he would also make sure that his mother and the rest of his family were taken care of, no matter what. He knew that it was going to be a long and difficult journey, but he was ready to face it head-on.

Over the next few weeks, John spent every spare moment when he wasn't working by his father's side, praying for his recovery and helping his mother with the bills and household tasks. It was a challenging time, but John found strength in the love and support of Hannah, who was always there for him and never once complained about the changes in their plans for the prom.

As his father condition slowly began to decline each day, John found himself reflecting on the lessons he had learned during this difficult time. He realized that he had taken his family for granted, and he vowed to be more grateful and supportive in the future. He also realized that he had to let go of his anger towards his father and try to understand the struggles he had faced in his own life. And most importantly, he realized that he had to stand up for himself and not let others, like Odell, bully and oppress him.

John didn't know if he could afford to go to the prom with all that has just happened. He would often think about Hannah by his side at the prom. John knew the night would be an experience to remember, full of dancing, laughter, and love. John walked Hannah home at the end of the night, he always felt a sense of hope and possibility for the future when they were together. He also knew that he still had a lot of work to do, but he was ready to face it with determination, courage, and resilience with Hannah by his side.

"A New Beginning"

As John and his mother left the hospital the next day, they both felt a sense of hope and determination. Despite the challenges they had faced, they were determined to move forward and make the most of their lives. John knew that he needed to take responsibility for his actions and make amends for the mistakes he had made. He also knew that he needed to be more understanding and supportive of his father, who was going through a difficult time.

As they walked home, John's mother told him about the steps his father was taking to turn his life around. He had stopped drinking, started attending meetings, and promised to build a better relationship with me and you. John was touched by his father's efforts and would be grateful if they would've been given a second chance.

As they entered their apartment, John felt a sense of hope and possibility. He knew that the road ahead would not be easy, but he was determined to make the most of every opportunity that came his way. John also couldn't help but think how exciting it would be to go to the prom with Hannah, but no matter what happens he was determined to excel in school and make a better life for himself and his family.

As he stared out his bedroom that night, watching all the typical mayhem on his street John felt a sense of peace and contentment. He knew that he had a long journey ahead of him, but he was ready to take on the challenges that lay ahead. Knowing that a new beginning was waiting for him just around the corner despite their struggles.

Despite the challenges he faced, John remained optimistic about his future and the possibility of a brighter tomorrow. He knew that with hard work and determination, he could overcome any obstacle that came his way. He was ready to take on the world and make a difference, not just for himself but for those around him.

As he drifted off to sleep that night, John couldn't help but feel a sense of hope and purpose, knowing that he had the strength and resilience to overcome any challenge that came his way. He was ready to chase his dreams and make a better life for himself and his loved ones. And he knew that no matter what, he would always have the love and support of his mother and Hannah to carry him through.

"The Night of the Dance: Pride and Perseverance"

As John stood in the hallway, anxiously waiting for his mother to leave out for a night on the town, he couldn't shake the feeling that he wouldn't be able to go to the prom. Despite how much he wanted to be there, he knew that they couldn't afford the expensive ticket and formal attire.

Just as his mother was about to leave, Kelly called him into the bedroom. She pulled him into a hug and said, "Son, I am so proud of you. Now, you be a gentleman and treat this girl right, you hear me?" John nodded, promising to be on his best behavior.

"Bedroom," Kelly said, pointing towards his room. Confused, John went into the bedroom and was met with a sight that took his breath away. Hanging on his closet door was a sleek white suit, with a pair of shiny dress shoes on the ground beneath it.

Overcome with emotion, John ran to his mother and hugged her tightly. "Thank you," he cried, tears streaming down his face. "You earned it, dear. Be happy," she replied, giving him a reassuring smile.

With a newfound sense of excitement and determination, John quickly got dressed in his new suit and shoes and made his way to Hannah's house. As he walked, he felt a surge of confidence wash over him. He was ready to make the most of this special night, and he knew that with his mother's support, anything was possible.

"A Night to Remember: John and Hannah's Dance"

As John approached Hannah's house, his nerves began to build. He had never been to a dance before, and he wasn't sure what to expect. But as soon as Hannah opened the door and he saw her standing there in a beautiful dress, all of his doubts melted away.

"Wow, you look...amazing," John stuttered, taking in Hannah's appearance. She blushed and replied, "Thank you. You look pretty sharp yourself, you clean up good John."

"What? This old thing?" John laughed, trying to play it cool. "Thanks Hannah. Ready to go?"

"Yes, lead the way," Hannah replied with a smile.

Since the dance was being held at the school, which was nearby, they decided to walk and enjoy the beautiful moonlit night. "It's nice out tonight, isn't it John?" Hannah said, taking in the sights and sounds around them.

"Yes it is, it looks as if there are more stars out than usual," John replied, gazing up at the clear sky.

"It really is beautiful," Hannah said, taking a deep breath of the crisp night air.

John, feeling bold, replied suggestively, "Yes, it really is. You know, I was really surprised when you asked me to the dance. You're one of the prettiest girls in school, you could have chosen anyone you wanted."

Hannah turned to him with a twinkle in her eye and said, "I did."

Dumbfounded and positively turning red, John closed his mouth and took Hannah's hand, and they walked to the school in silence for the remainder of their journey. As they arrived at the dance, John couldn't believe that he was there with Hannah, and he knew that it was going to be a night to remember.

"The School Dance: A Night of Celebration and Confidence"

The school dance was a festive and elaborate affair, with decorations and snacks filling the room. At first, no one was dancing, and the students were awkward and shy.

John took Hannah by the hand and led her to the center of the dance floor, showing her that it was okay to be the first ones to start dancing. Despite her initial resistance, Hannah began to follow John's lead and they started dancing together.

As John and Hannah continued to dance, more and more students joined in, including the jocks and sports enthusiasts who were usually more confident on the dance floor. They showed off their moves and encouraged their dates to do the same.

The energy in the room grew as more and more students started dancing, and everyone was having a great time. John and Hannah were surrounded by eager dancers who were now loose and ready to show their moves.

John felt confident and proud as he danced with Hannah at the school dance. He had overcome his feelings of shame and embarrassment about his financial struggles and was able to fully enjoy the moment. For John, the school dance was a night of celebration and confidence, and he knew that it was one he would always remember.

"The Parking Lot Rendezvous: A Moment of Decision"

As the DJ played slow songs, John and Hannah took to the dance floor. They respectfully embraced each other and moved to the rhythm of the music, both wondering if they should take the next step and share a kiss.

As they danced, they couldn't help but feel a strong connection between them. They were both nervous, but they also knew that they wanted to be together.

When Hannah and John returned to the table at different times, they each found a note inviting them to meet in the parking lot after the dance. John headed out to the parking lot, waiting for Hannah.

As he stood there in the cool night air, John couldn't help but feel a sense of anticipation and excitement. He knew that this was a moment of decision, and he wasn't sure what he wanted to do.

Should he follow his heart and go for it, or should he play it safe and keep things between them platonic? As he stood there, lost in thought, Hannah appeared at his side, looking up at him with a hopeful gaze.

John knew in that moment what he wanted, and he leaned down to kiss Hannah, sealing their fate as a couple. As they embraced in the moonlit parking lot, they knew that they had found something special in each other, and they were ready to take on the world together.

"The Slick Trick: A Lesson in Standing Up for Yourself and Being Honest"

Just before Hannah left the parking lot, while walking through the door, she was drenched in green slime. She accused John of being the one who set up the bucket of slime, but he denied it, saying he didn't do it.

As the rain came down in sheets, Hannah's hair and clothes was drenched in bright green slime. She immediately turned to John, her eyes blazing with anger and hurt. "You did this," she accused him, her voice shaking with emotion. "You set me up!"

John couldn't believe what he was hearing. He had been having such a great time at the prom, dancing with Hannah and enjoying the night. Now, everything was falling apart. "No, Hannah, I didn't do this," he protested, shaking his head. "I would never do something like this to you."

But Hannah wasn't listening. She was too upset and hurt to hear John's words of innocence. "I can't believe I trusted you," she spat out, before turning and storming off, leaving John standing alone and bewildered. Hannah, hurt and upset, told John she never wanted to see him again and to just stay away from her.

As he watched Hannah go, John couldn't help but feel a sense of despair wash over him. He had always cared about Hannah deeply, and the thought of losing her was devastating. But just as he was about to give into his despair, something caught his eye.

Odell, the school bully, was sitting in the gym teacher's car, holding up a notebook paper and pen. As John watched in shock, Odell confessed to being the one who left the notes at the table and caused the misunderstanding between John and Hannah.

37

Tears streamed down John's cheeks as he realized the full extent of Odell's cruelty. He had been played for a fool, and the thought was almost too much to bear. As Odell laughed and drove off with his date, John started to chase the car but the car was to fast. He had finally had enough of Odells bullying and was ready to destroy him. But John was left standing alone, his heart heavy with grief and regret.

Feeling lost and alone, John slowly began to make his way home, his mind racing with thoughts of what he could have done differently. He wished he had stood up to Odell in the past and been more open with Hannah about his feelings rather than just keeping his feelings inside. He also knew that relying on his anger and emotions had gotten him into trouble in the past, and he couldn't risk ruining his chances of escaping poverty and getting into a good college.

Despite the heartbreak, John knew that he had to be strong and move forward. He made a promise to himself to be more assertive and to stand up for what he believed in, no matter the consequences. He also vowed to be more honest and open with his feelings, even if it meant facing rejection or hurt again.

Through the pain and heartache of the prom, John learned valuable lessons about standing up for himself and being true to his feelings. He hoped that he would never make the same mistakes again, and that he would have the courage to face the future with a new sense of confidence and purpose.

"The Breaking Point"

John stood in front of a car, his heart heavy with grief and despair. He couldn't believe what had happened. Everything had fallen apart in a matter of minutes. He thought about all the hardships he had faced: the guilt he felt over his father's accident, growing up in poverty, being teased at school, and being bullied by Odell. He still had not heard from his teacher about accepting his lead project and wondered how it would impact his future. And now, the one bright spot in his life, Hannah, wanted nothing to do with him.

He was overwhelmed by the struggles and challenges of his life, and he felt like he couldn't recover from this latest blow. Desperate to see Hannah and explain the situation, John raced to her house, hoping to find some kind of resolution. But when he arrived, he was met with rejection.

Hannah assured John of his innocence in the hurtful prank, but she couldn't ignore his lack of confidence in standing up to bullying and reaching his full potential. She felt it would be best they would go their separate ways so John can focus on who he truly wanted to become.

As they prepared to part ways, Hanna emphasized the importance of personal growth and courage. She hoped John would find the strength to overcome obstacles and discover his true self. In their bittersweet farewell, Hannah expressed uncertainty about the future but held onto hope for their enduring friendship. John did not understand that their separate journeys would possibly lead to self-discovery.

Hanna's words echoed unspoken dreams and aspirations. She believed in John's ability to overcome adversity and urged him to embrace his destiny with determination. Although Hannah, wanted the best for John he was still hurt, leaving him feeling even more alone and helpless.

Convinced that his life was over, John felt a surge of anger and grief wash over him. He couldn't take it anymore. He was sick of feeling powerless, sick of being pushed around and mistreated. And so, in a moment of desperation, he made a decision. John stood in front of the car that one of Hannah's neighbors had accidentally left running. The neighbor had forgotten her phone so she ran back into the house. John's heart was heavy with grief and despair. He couldn't believe what had just happened. Everything had fallen apart in a matter of minutes. He thought about all the hardships he had faced: the guilt he felt over his father's accident, growing up in poverty, being teased at school, and being bullied by Odell. He still had not heard from his teacher about accepting his lead project and wondered how it would impact his future. And now, the one bright spot in his life, Hannah, wanted nothing to do with him.

"The Wake-Up Call"

A fragile anchor in a sea of instability, John succumbed to his wavering psyche and seized hold of the neighbor's abandoned car, its engine still humming with life. As he careened through the streets, reckless abandon gripping the wheel, anger devoured his thoughts, eclipsing any glimmer of hope. Yet, on the precipice of surrendering to his innermost despair, he found solace in a simple act—he closed his eyes, seeking respite from the tempest within, yearning for a sliver of serenity to emerge from the depths of his troubled mind.

Suddenly, there was a loud crash. The stolen car had hit a light post in front of John's house, and smoke was rising from the hood. John felt a sharp pain in his head, and when he touched his temple, he saw that his hand was covered in blood. Dazed and confused, he tried to climb out of the car, but his legs felt like jelly. Just then he fell to the ground and blacked out.

When he woke up, he found himself in a hospital bed, with a nurse by his side. She told him that he had been in an accident, and that his mother had rushed him to the hospital. John couldn't believe what had happened - it was like a bad dream. But as he listened to the nurse, he realized that it was all too real.

When his mother, Kelly, entered the room, she hugged him tightly, tears streaming down her face. "Don't scare me like that again," she whispered, holding him close.

As John listened to his mother, he realized how lucky he was to be alive. He also realized that he had been selfish, focusing on his own pain and problems and forgetting about the people he loved. He made a resolution in that moment - he was going to dedicate his life to his mother, and to make her proud. He was going to be strong, to stand up for himself, and to fight for the life he deserved. And as he looked into his mother's eyes, he knew that he was ready to take on whatever challenges lay ahead.

"The Road to Redemption"

Yet with the knowledge of Hannah's lingering discontent, John's heart urged him forward, compelling him to extend his hand toward her, a fervent attempt to elucidate the transformative path he had embarked upon. In his impassioned plea, he sought to convey that he had shed the skin of his former self, embracing a newfound essence that resonated with the man she yearned for him to become. Though understanding her longing, he longed to bridge the chasm between their souls, hoping to illuminate the depths of his evolution.

He begged for her forgiveness and promised to never let anything like that happen again in the future. He understood that she was hurt, but he couldn't help but want to make things right between them.

Although Hannah was no longer upset and confused about what had really happened that night, she told John that she wanted him to focus on himself and find the strength to become the person he was really meant to be. She said that for now, she just wanted to be left alone. John's soul was crushed as he sat in the park, feeling depressed and overwhelmed by feelings of pain and misery.

But despite the heartache, John refused to give up. He knew that he had made mistakes, but he was determined to make things right. He focused on his education and his future after high school, taking responsibility for his actions and trying to make amends wherever he could. He also worked on improving himself and making better decisions in the future.

John, once imprisoned in the juvenile center for his reckless car heist, a wild drive that defied reason, has since sought redemption. He toiled away with community work, bearing the weight of his misdeeds, and engaged in introspection, meeting someone who tended to his fragile mental health. This endeavor, a balm to his troubled soul, succeeded in absolving his transgressions, allowing him to forge ahead unburdened. But the grandest marvel of all resides in the transformation it birthed within John, as he pieced together the fragments of his shattered past and erected a new foundation for his destiny to unfurl.

Through it all, John remained determined to rebuild his relationships and be a better person. He knew that it wouldn't be easy, but he was willing to do whatever it took to earn back Hannah's trust and love. And as he waited patiently for her response, he held onto hope that one day, things would be right between them again.

"The New Beginning"

As John moved forward, he was determined to make the most of every day. He knew that he had been given a second chance, and he was determined to make the most of it. He focused on rebuilding his life and making his mother proud, working hard to be a better person and to make a difference in the world.

He also made an effort to be more understanding and compassionate towards others, knowing that everyone makes mistakes and that it's important to forgive and move on. And as he looked towards the future, he was filled with hope and optimism. He knew that he had the strength and determination to overcome any challenges that came his way and to build the life that he wanted.

John's efforts to make amends and improve himself paid off. He was able to get into a great college with a full scholarship, and he was thrilled to have the opportunity to build a new life for himself. He was grateful for the second chance that he had been given, and he vowed to make the most of it.

As he looked towards the future, John was excited to see what it held. He was determined to make the most of every opportunity that came his way, and he knew that with hard work and determination, he could achieve anything he set his mind to. He was ready to take on the world, and he knew that he had the strength and courage to face whatever challenges lay ahead.

15 years later: 15 years of Dedication

John had always known that becoming a doctor would be a long and difficult journey, but he had never let that deter him from his dream. As he sat in his office, he couldn't help but reflect on all that he had accomplished in the past 15 years.

Discovering his true essence held great significance for John. Yet another crucial factor in John's triumphant journey was the survival and recovery of his father after the accident. This positive turn of events granted John the ability to genuinely forgive his father and embark on a new path. Moreover, John was keenly aware that clinging to silence and concealing his emotions would inevitably lead to his own destruction. He understood that suppressing those feelings would also inflict harm upon his mental well-being. Seeking counseling, John found solace and acquired the necessary tools to navigate those sentiments with greater efficacy.

It had been a hard road, filled with long hours, sleepless nights, and endless studying, but John had never given up. And finally, his hard work had paid off. He had become a successful doctor, respected by his colleagues and loved by his patients.

But as he looked up to see his mother enter the office, John realized that the journey had not been easy for her either. "Mom! Wow, to be honest, I was expecting someone else," he said, feeling a sudden wave of guilt wash over him as he realized how little time he had been making for his loved ones.

"Yes, I know," his mother replied, a hint of sadness in her voice. "Since you started working, you have no time for me."

John immediately reached out to reassure her, feeling a pang of guilt for neglecting his mother. "No, Mom, don't be like that. How are you?"

"Wonderful," she replied, a smile returning to her face. "Are we still on for dinner?"

"Yes, of course," John replied, relieved that he could make it up to his mother. "As soon as I finish up here, Mom. How's your new job, by the way? And have you settled into your new house okay?"

"Yes, thank you so much for the house, son," his mother replied, a grateful smile on her face. "It's a lot bigger than I thought it would be, but I still love it. Thank you."

As John spent the rest of the evening with his mother, he couldn't help but feel a sense of pride and accomplishment. He had dedicated the past 15 to becoming the best doctor he could be, and now he was reaping the rewards. But he also realized that his journey had not been solely his own. He had the support and love of his mother and other loved ones, and for that he was truly grateful.

The Unexpected Encounter

John wrapped up his work and prepared to leave with his mother, feeling a sense of anticipation for the dinner plans they had made with his father and wife. "Well, Mom, I think I'm just about finished here. Ready to go?" he asked.

"Yes, I am," his mother replied, a smile on her face. "Lead the way, John."

Just as John was about to leave, he was interrupted by an unexpected request. "Mr. Anderson, you have another client," Michelle said who was John's medical assistant, drawing John's attention away from his mother.

"It's the end of the day and we're closed for the evening. Can the person schedule an appointment for tomorrow?" John asked, hoping to wrap up his work and stick to his plans.

"He says it's important, sir," Michelle replied, a note of urgency in her voice.

John sighed, knowing that he couldn't turn away a client in need. "Alright, send him in, thank you, Michelle," he said, reluctantly agreeing to meet with the late client.

As John's mother left the office, she reminded him not to be too long. "Don't be too long, son," she said. "Your father and I made a reservation for four of us at your favorite restaurant, and your father can't wait to spend some time with you and your wife again. Take care of your business and just let me know when you're ready. I'll be waiting for you in the lobby."

John nodded, feeling a mix of excitement and stress as he prepared to meet with his unexpected visitor. He knew that he had to balance his responsibilities as a doctor with his desire to spend time with his loved ones, and he hoped that this meeting wouldn't take too long.

51

A Rekindled Relationship

John sat at his desk, eyeing the poorly-dressed man with who had just walked into his office. Something about him seemed familiar, but John couldn't quite place it. He was slow to anger and rage, and he couldn't help but feel a sense of darkness emanating from the man's presence.

"Thank you for seeing me," the man said, taking off his cap and clutching it between his hands as he sat down. "I need your help, my daughter is deathly ill and you were recommended as the best in your field for an unbelievable low rate and helping those in need."

John's heart went out to the man, and he immediately offered his help. "What's the illness?" he asked.

"I don't know, I was hoping you could take a look at her," the man replied, desperation etched on his face.

"What's her name?" John asked, already reaching for his notes and pen.

"Sarah James," the man answered, his eyes full of hope and fear.

John was surprised to hear the name James, as he used to know someone by that name who had tormented him in middle school. "I wonder where he is now," John whispered to himself.

"Across from you," the man replied, a hint of a smile on his face. "It's me...Odell."

John was shocked to realize that the man sitting across from him was his childhood bully. Despite his initial surprise, he had learned the lesson of forgiveness after the accident involving his father and was able to react calmly to the unexpected reunion.

As they sat and caught up, John couldn't help but feel a sense of shame and embarrassment emanating from Odell. He could tell that the man was desperate, and he knew that he probably wouldn't have come to him for help if he had any other options. John couldn't turn his back on a child in need, and he decided to offer his help despite their rocky past.

Just as they were discussing the details of Sarah's treatment, there was a knock at the door. In walked a beautiful woman with curly brown hair and green eyes, who was evidently pregnant. "I hope this isn't a bad time, honey," she said, a warm smile on her face.

"Hannah, sweetheart," John replied, standing up to give her a hug. "Kiss. I'm almost done, I'll just be a minute."

Odell was shocked and excited to see that John and Hannah had worked things out and were now married, even after the prank he had played on Hannah in high school. Odell attempted to apologize to Hannah and John for the prank, but they assured him that forgiveness had already been granted long ago. They understood that dwelling on past grievances would only serve to divide and weaken them, rather than empowering them as individuals or as a collective. They recognized the transformative power of releasing the burdens of the past, enabling them to move forward with strength and unity. Through forgiveness, they discovered a newfound resilience, no longer confined by the shadows of their shared history. Whether together or apart, they stood tall and unwavering, fortified by the liberating act of forgiveness. They embraced the truth that destruction held no answers, realizing that love and understanding were the paths to genuine joy and harmony.

Hannah, in the manner of Langston Hughes, conveyed her thoughts to Odell. Initially, she found herself upset with John, and even with Odell, on that fateful day. The emotions of embarrassment and anger engulfed her young and bewildered mind. In her confusion, she believed John to be lacking in strength and confidence for not standing up to the challenges he faced over the years. But as time passed, Hannah came to understand that bravery transcends mere physical might. It encompasses the resilience to confront the forces that conspire to demolish one's dreams. The true measure of a person lies in their unwavering determination and unwavering focus on their aspirations, regardless of the obstacles they encounter. It was in witnessing this inner strength within John that Hannah knew he was the one for her. She beamed with pride as he exhibited his unwavering determination to move forward. And so, after several years of nurturing their friendship and deepening their love through courtship, they resolved to embark on the journey of matrimony together. Still, Odell was grateful that they accepted his apology. As the three of them sat and caught up, John couldn't help but feel grateful for the unexpected reunion and the chance to move forward from the past.

"A New Beginning: John and Odell's Journey to Forgiveness and Healing"

John sat back down at his desk as Hannah left the office. He turned to Odell and said, "If your daughter is deathly ill, and she may be in need of emergency attention. I would like to see her first thing tomorrow morning to ensure she gets the proper care. Can you come by at around 7am?"

Odell's face lit up with hope and gratitude. "Yes, yes I can. Thank you so much," he replied, his voice shaking with emotion.

"It's nothing," John said, trying to downplay his own generosity. He knew how much this meant to Odell, and he was determined to do everything in his power to help Sarah get better.

As they left the office and headed to dinner with his mother, wife, and father, John couldn't shake the feeling that this was a new beginning for all of them. He was grateful to have the opportunity to help Sarah and her father, and he was looking forward to seeing them first thing in the morning to assess her condition and determine the best course of treatment.

The next day, John ran every test he could think of until he was finally able to uncover the cause of Sarah's illness. Odell stood vigilantly by her side, half afraid that John might seek revenge on his daughter for past wrongdoings. However, John took very good care of Sarah after discovering she had malaria, putting her needs before any personal feelings he may have had towards Odell. He knew that this was a chance to start fresh and build a new relationship with his former bully. And as Sarah's health improved, John couldn't help but feel hopeful for the future.

57

"Starting Over: The Renewal of John and Odell's Friendship"

Odell trailed after John, emerging from the confines of the recovery room, his heart laden with the weight of shame. "John!" he called out, cautious to avoid physical contact. "Yes?" John responded, pivoting to meet his gaze. "I'm at a loss for words to express my gratitude. How can I repay you?" Odell pleaded, desperation resonating in his voice. "Ensure your daughter is spared from the echoes of my own past, that she blossoms into the formidable woman her potential foretells," John uttered, his words infused with profound significance. "I promise you, I shall fulfill that duty, and I offer my deepest gratitude once more," Odell conveyed, his heart swelling with appreciation for the kindness and wisdom bestowed upon him by John's altruistic spirit.

"Listen, I'll be off this weekend. Would you like to get a drink and catch up?" John asked, a hint of a smile on his lips. "That would be great," Odell said, relieved to have the chance to reconnect with John. "Don't be too happy about it. You're buying," John said, laughing. "You've got it, Doc," Odell replied, grateful for the opportunity to make amends and rebuild their friendship.

Despite the rocky start, John and Odell were able to put the past behind them and focus on the present and future. They spent the evening catching up and rebuilding their relationship over drinks. It was a new beginning for both of them, as they were able to move past the pain and hurt of the past and forge a new friendship. They were grateful for the chance to start fresh and make amends for the mistakes of their youth.

As they sat in the cozy bar, Langston Hughes' poetry rhythms played in their minds, evoking memories of past struggles and triumphs. John couldn't help but wonder if Odell's bullying was a test to see if he would succumb to the forces that attempt to destroy one's dreams. They both knew the road ahead wouldn't be easy, but they were determined to face it together as friends and allies. The drama of their past was behind them, and they looked forward to a bright future filled with hope and possibility. With hard work and determination, they could overcome any obstacle and create a better world for themselves and those around them. With hearts full of gratitude and hope, John and Odell raised their glasses in a toast to a new beginning.

"Redemption and Second Chances:"

As the evening came to a close, John and Odell bid each other farewell, looking forward to the future and all that it held. They were excited to see what the future would bring, and were grateful to have each other's friendship and support as they moved forward.

Inspired by their newfound bond and the desire to give back to their community, Odell and John decided to take action. They worked tirelessly to build a community mentorship center in their old neighborhood, providing support and guidance to young people who had faced bullying and other challenges.

Their hard work paid off, and the center quickly became a beacon of hope and support for countless young people in the community. Odell and John were proud of the positive impact they were making, and were grateful to have the opportunity to give back and make a difference.

As the years passed, John and Hannah's family grew, with the addition of a healthy baby boy. Their marriage wasn't always easy, but they were able to make it work through love, understanding, and forgiveness. John's father also survived his accident and was able to mend his relationship with his son and Kelly.

Odell was enlightened by a profound lesson interwoven with the strands of bullying, violence, and their potential to alter the course of his daughter's and John's life. In the embrace of gratitude, Odell cherished the fact that John possessed a forgiving heart, readily extending his hand to assist in the rescue of his beloved child. This invaluable insight has become an indelible part of Odell's essence, one he is certain to pass down to his offspring and share with others in his community.

Meanwhile, Odell's stepfather Kevin eventually faced consequences for his abuse with Odell's mom and child abuse, and was bullied every day by his new cellmate. He learned a valuable lesson on the harmful effects of bullying but was determined to turn his life around when he gets out of prison.

As John looked back on the journey he had taken, he couldn't help but feel grateful for the second chance he had been given. He had learned the importance of forgiveness and moving forward, and was determined to make the most of his new beginning.

In the style of Langston Hughes, John's story of redemption and second chances was told through powerful poetry and prose, capturing the hearts and minds of readers everywhere. It was a story of hope and resilience, and one that would be celebrated and remembered for generations to come. And so, with a heart full of gratitude and a bright future ahead, John looked forward to what the future held, knowing that with hard work and determination, anything was possible.

61

THE END

Best ways to seek help suffering from depression and suicidal thoughts

If you are experiencing depression and suicidal thoughts, it is important to seek help as soon as possible. Here are some steps you can take:

1. Reach out to a mental health professional. A therapist or counselor can help you work through your feelings and develop coping strategies.
2. Talk to a trusted friend or family member. Sharing your thoughts and feelings with someone you trust can provide emotional support and help you feel less alone.
3. Call a suicide hotline. There are many hotlines available that provide confidential, 24/7 support to people in crisis. Some options include the National Suicide Prevention Lifeline (1-800-273-TALK), the Crisis Text Line (text HOME to 741741), and the International Association for Suicide Prevention (1-800-SUICIDE).
4. Seek support from a support group. Joining a support group for people with depression or those who have experienced suicidal thoughts can be a helpful way to connect with others who understand what you are going through

It's important to remember that you are not alone and that there is help available. It may be difficult to reach out for help, but it can be the first step towards feeling better and getting the support you need.

Best ways to handle bullying in school or at home

Bullying can be a difficult and distressing experience, and it is important to take steps to address it. Here are some steps you can take to handle bullying in school or at home:

1. Reach out for support: It can be helpful to speak to a trusted adult, such as a teacher, counselor, or parent, about the bullying you are experiencing. They can provide you with support and guidance on how to handle the situation.
2. If available, visit your school's website for trusted guidance on how to handle bullying in your school.
3. Stand up for yourself: If you feel safe and comfortable doing so, try standing up to the bully in a calm and assertive way. For example, you could say something like "I don't like it when you talk to me that way. Please stop."
4. Use humor: Sometimes, bullies behave the way they do to get a reaction from their victims. If you can use humor to defuse the situation, the bully may lose interest.
5. Ignore the bully: In some cases, ignoring the bully may be the best course of action. This can be especially effective if the bully is seeking attention.
6. Stay away from the bully: If you can, try to avoid situations where you might encounter the bully. This might mean taking a different route to class or avoiding certain areas of the school or home.
7. Get involved: One way to combat bullying is to get involved in activities that promote kindness and inclusion, such as starting a bullying prevention club at school or participating in community service projects.
8. Seek professional help: If you are struggling to cope with bullying or if the situation is severe, it may be helpful to seek the support of a mental health professional. They can provide you with coping strategies and help you address any related emotional issues.

Printed in the United States
by Baker & Taylor Publisher Services